PUFFIN BOOKS

THE THING IN THE WOODS

When Jenny and her brother Bill are walking their dog in the woods, they come across a very tall, very thin and very frightened Thing. It certainly isn't human, but what exactly is it? The Thing is very hungry, but can they possibly take it to the local Chinese take-away! Jenny and Bill make friends with the Thing, and try to help it speak English; but their friends Johnny and Ada Connor are not impressed by their stories, in fact they just don't believe that the Thing exists. When Johnny and Ada secretly follow Jenny and Bill down to the woods, they are in for a very big surprise!

Vivien Alcock grew up in Sussex and worked as a commercial artist before beginning to write. Since then she has written many highly-praised stories for children. She is married with one daughter, and lives in London with her husband and their dog Ben, and cat Charlie.

D0552912

The Thing in the Woods

VIVIEN ALCOCK

Illustrated by Sally Holmes

PUFFIN BOOKS

PUFFIN BOOKS

Published by the Penguin Group
Penguin Books Ltd, 27 Wrights Lane, London W8 5TZ, England
Penguin Books USA Inc., 375 Hudson Street, New York, New York 10014, USA
Penguin Books Australia Ltd, Ringwood, Victoria, Australia
Penguin Books Canada Ltd, 10 Alcorn Avenue, Toronto, Ontario, Canada M4V 3B2
Penguin Books (NZ) Ltd, 182–190 Wairau Road, Auckland 10, New Zealand

Penguin Books Ltd, Registered Offices: Harmondsworth, Middlesex, England

First published by Hamish Hamilton Children's Books 1989
Published in Puffin Books 1991
3 5 7 9 10 8 6 4

Printed in England by Clays Ltd, St Ives plc
Filmset in Baskerville (Linotron 202)

For Frances and Piers

Chapter 1

THERE WAS A Thing in the woods, a most peculiar Thing. Nobody knew it was there. Nobody had seen it come. All night it lay where it had fallen. A small sound came from it – eek, eek, eek – like a branch in the wind.

In the morning the sun shone through the leaves. The Thing blinked and sat up.

Its head hurt. Where was it? It didn't know. Who was it? It couldn't

remember. Its head beat like a drum, making it hard to think.

The Thing patted its pockets. Then it stood up and shook itself. A small yellow book fell to the ground.

It picked up the book and turned the pages.

"Ko gogga sta," it muttered. "My name is . . . my name is . . ."

It was no good. It could not find its name anywhere in the book. Without a name, it did not feel like a person any more. It was just a Thing in the woods. It began to cry.

"Eek, eek, eek, ah-hoo-oo!" it howled.

Birds flew away in fright. A dog

began to bark in a garden nearby. The Thing stopped crying, and listened. Its eyes brightened. It wasn't alone in the world after all. Quickly it turned the pages in its little book till it found the words it wanted.

"CAN YOU HELP ME, PLEASE?" it bellowed.

Then it waited in the woods for someone to come.

In the nearby garden, the dog was still barking. His name was Fortissimo

because he was so loud. The children called him Mo for short. He was a great hairy haystack of a dog, with a bark like a brass hammer on a tin tray.

Jenny Clarke was lying on the grass with her hands over her ears, reading a book. Her young brother Bill was pushing a model car round a clump of daisies. They took no notice of Fortissimo.

He was always barking. He barked at the postman and the milkman and the dustbin men. He barked at the cat next door. He seemed to think they wanted to know every time a bird flew over their garden or a bee rifled their roses. Their mother said he was so stupid he couldn't tell a burglar from a butterfly.

"Shut up, Mo," everybody kept saying.

Now his bark had become shrill and offended. He was trying to tell the children something important. There was a strange Thing in the woods. He had caught its faint, peculiar scent on the wind. He had heard its odd, hoarse shriek. He thought the children ought to know about it. After all, it might be dangerous.

He barked even more loudly.

Mrs Clarke came whirling out of the

house, with a dab of flour on her nose
and an angry flush on her cheeks.

"Are you two deaf?" she demanded.
"That wretched dog's been barking his
head off for hours. How you can just
sit there and do nothing . . . Has he
been out for his walk yet? Jenny, I'm
talking to you!"

She prodded her daughter with her

toe. Jenny looked up and took her hands away from her ears.

"What, Mum?"

"Has Mo been out for his walk yet?"

"Don't think so. It's not my turn, it's Bill's."

"Oo, it isn't! I took him yesterday."

"No, you didn't – "

"I don't care whose turn it is," their mother said. "You both wanted a dog. I didn't. So you can both take him out. No, not later, Jenny. Now. This very minute. And not just up to the sweet shop either. Take him down to the woods where he can have a good run and tire himself out."

Fortissimo recognised the word
'woods'. He began jumping up and
down in great excitement, telling them
at the top of his voice that he was
prepared to fight the Thing in the
woods, if he had to. But he rather
hoped it wouldn't be necessary.
Although he was big and noisy, he was
only a young dog; a gentle, friendly
dog who had never bitten anything

larger than a dog biscuit in his life. To be honest, he felt rather nervous. He couldn't help hoping that the Thing, whatever it was, would not be too big.

Chapter 2

THE TREES HUDDLED together, shutting out the sunlight and the sounds of the city. The woods had once been part of a great forest where kings had hunted and outlaws hidden. Now it had dwindled to a green patch on the outskirts, a home for birds and squirrels, and a place to walk dogs.

"You can let him off the lead, Bill," Jenny said.

Fortissimo ran backwards and

forwards over the ground like a
darning needle. He sniffed every tree.
He sniffed the earth. Then he raised

his head and sniffed the air. Funny. He
couldn't smell the strange Thing any
longer. Perhaps it had gone. Perhaps

the wind was blowing the other way. Perhaps the Thing could smell *him* now. That was a nasty thought.

"What's the matter with Fortissimo?" Bill asked. "He doesn't seem to want to run about any longer. D'you think he's all right?"

Jenny looked at the dog, who was keeping close to their heels now.

"I dunno," she said. "He does seem a bit – " She broke off.

Fortissimo had stopped. He was staring at a clump of bushes. His nose twitched twice. Then the hair rose up on his back, making him look twice the dog he really was. Unfortunately the effect was ruined by the fact that he was trembling with alarm.

"Eek, eek, eek!"

"What was that?" Jenny whispered.

The Thing stepped out from behind a bush.

It stood on the path in front of them. Very tall. Very thin. Its eyes were a dusty purple, like plums. Its hair was green and sharp, like holly leaves. Its skin was grey and it wore a green fur coat. Each bare foot had four toes, three in front and one at the back, like a bird's.

Fortissimo began to bark. Nervously
at first, then the sound of his own voice
gave him courage. His bark became
louder and louder, till it rang out like
an iron hammer on a tin drum.

"Eek, eek, eek!" the Thing cried.

It ran up a tree like a giant spider
and clung to a branch. It was

17

quivering. Tears fell from its face like rain from the sky.

"Why, it's frightened," Jenny said, and felt braver.

Bill tugged at her hand. He was younger than Jenny. He thought they ought to go home. Now.

Fortissimo began jumping up the tree. The Thing whimpered, and shook so much that leaves fell down on their heads like green confetti. Jenny put Fortissimo on his lead and told him to be quiet. He grumbled at the back of his throat and looked offended. Then he sat down with his back towards them.

"Don't cry," Jenny said to the Thing. "We won't hurt you."

The Thing sniffed.

"Gop wagga binka bobs," it babbled.

"What did it say?" Bill whispered, holding Jenny's hand tight.

"I don't know," she said. "I don't think it's English."

The Thing sat up on the branch and began to pat its green fur coat. Then it took a small yellow book from its pocket. It turned the pages.

"Can you help me? Good morning. Please. Thank you," it said.

It had a high, creaking sort of voice, like a bird with a sore throat. They stared at it in surprise.

"Good morning," Jenny said at last.

The Thing slid down the tree. Jenny held tight to Fortissimo's collar. Bill held tight to her other hand. The Thing was much worse now that it was so near them. It stank like burnt mushrooms and old socks.

"What is it?" Bill whispered.

19

The Thing heard him. It smiled and said, "What is this? What is that?"

"What is what?" Jenny asked.

"This," it said, and pointed to itself with a finger as thin as a twig.

"Don't you know?" she asked, surprised.

It shook its head. Then it pointed to Bill. "What is that?"

"I'm a boy," Bill said.

"I'm a boy?" the Thing asked hopefully.

"No, you're not."

It pointed at Jenny, but she shook her head.

"I don't think you're a girl either," she said. "At least, you're not like any girl I've ever seen before. Sorry."

The Thing looked upset. Tears filled its purple eyes, so that they shone like wet plums. It began hitting itself quite hard on the chest, crying, "What is that? What is that?"

"We don't know," Jenny said nervously. "We don't know what you are. Do we, Bill?"

They tried to walk away but it came with them, saying, "Can you help me? Please. Thank you. Excuse me."

Bill pulled Jenny's hand. He stood on tiptoe and whispered in her ear.

"It looks a bit like a tree on legs."

"A tree?" the Thing asked. Its ears must've been very sharp. "My name is a tree?"

Jenny was about to say no, when she had an idea.

"You could be a tree," she said. "Only you must put your feet down into the ground. Like that." She pointed to the roots of a tree.

The Thing didn't understand. It looked puzzled.

"Like this," Bill said, showing it.

"Ah," the Thing said. It wriggled its toes into the earth.

"That's right. Now hold up your arms. Like this."

The Thing held up its arms obediently.

It really did look very like a tree now. Its hair seemed to be growing bushier, as green and glossy as holly. Its grey arms and legs were as thin and knobbly as branches, and its green fur coat might easily have been moss. Only its face with its large plum-coloured eyes and big mouth was wrong for a tree.

"Now turn round," Jenny said. "*Turn*. Like this."

"Ah, turn," the Thing said. It nodded wisely, and turned round to face the tree behind it.

"Hullo. How are you? Good morning very well. Thank you," it said.

The tree said nothing. After all, it was only a tree.

"Hullo! How are you? Good morning!" the Thing shouted.

Jenny had intended to creep away with Bill as soon as the Thing's back was turned. But Fortissimo would not come. He sat on the ground as heavy as a rock, and stared at the Thing. Funny sort of tree. Never seen one like it before. He got up, and towing Jenny behind him, went to sniff at its ankles.

"No! Don't!" she shouted, trying to pull Fortissimo away.

23

24

She was too late. Fortissimo had lifted his leg.

"EEK! EEK! EEK!" the Thing screamed, leaping up into the air.

Its purple eyes blazed. They seemed to spin round in its face like Catherine

wheels. Its stiff hair bristled and gave
off green sparks. Its mouth opened as
wide as a chalk pit. It looked very
angry indeed.

Bill and Jenny fled, pulling
Fortissimo with them.

Chapter 3

THEY RAN AND RAN. Jenny's legs ached. She had a pain in her side, and her breath came short and fast. With one hand she held on to the end of Fortissimo's lead; with the other she dragged Bill behind her.

Her hair bounced around her head and fell across her face, blinding her. She tripped on a root and put out a hand to save herself from landing on her nose. Not having three hands, she

had to let something go. She let go of
the dog's lead.

Fortissimo went off like a yellow
streak of light. He shot round the
corner in a swirl of dead leaves. Then
he was gone.

"He's run away!" Bill said, his voice
heavy with disbelief. "He's left us."

"Yes." Jenny got slowly to her feet
and looked round. She could see
nothing but trees.

"Mo! Mo! Fortissimo!" Bill shrieked.
He put two fingers to his mouth and
whistled.

"He won't come back," Jenny said
bitterly. "At the rate he was going,
he'll be home by now."

"He's a coward," Bill said angrily,
blinking his eyes and sniffing. "I never
thought he'd leave us. I thought he
loved us."

"Never mind. Let's go home." Jenny looked back once more. Nothing but trees. She listened. A woodpecker tapping somewhere. A small wind playing in the leaves. A sudden clap of wings as a scatter of pigeons flew up into the air. A loud rustling, coming nearer . . .

The Thing came bounding up the path through the trees. It was lifting its knobbly knees very high, like a horse trotting. To their surprise, it ran right past them, up the path and out of sight.

They stared after it.

"Where's it going?" Bill asked.

"I don't know."

"Do you think it saw us?"

"It must've done."

"What shall we do?"

Jenny had no idea, but she didn't

want Bill to know this. She was older
than he was. She had to look after him.
  "We'll wait for a bit," she said.
  "What for?"

"To get our breath back – " she
broke off. "What's that?"

It was Fortissimo. He came racing
round the corner and slid to a stop in

front of them, panting and wagging his
tail.

"He's come back!" Bill cried
joyfully. He knelt down and put his
arms round the dog's neck. "Good old
Mo, you came back."

"I expect something was chasing
him," Jenny said.

"It wasn't that! Don't be horrible.
He came back to protect us, didn't
you, Mo?" Bill asked. Mo licked his
cheek. Then he leaped out of Bill's
embrace and stood on the path, staring
towards the corner. He began to growl
at the back of his throat.

The Thing came strolling round the

corner, holding its yellow book in its hands. It stopped when it saw them.

"Good morning, good afternoon," it said politely. "Where is the bus, the train, the airport? Please very much."

Jenny stared at it. It looked different. It had smoothed down its bushy green hair, and undone the top three buttons of its coat to show a lavender shirt beneath. It was almost as if it hoped they'd think it was a new Thing. One they'd never met before. One nobody could possibly mistake for a tree.

It must need our help badly, Jenny thought, and felt sorry for it.

"Where do you want to go?" she asked.

The Thing turned a page in its book. Then another. Then another.

"I do not know," it said, and began

to cry again. "Eek, eek, eek."

"Can I see?" Jenny asked, holding out her hand for the book.

The Thing gave it to her. It was an odd book. The pages were made of some thin, slippery stuff like silk. On one side of each page, there were squiggles, as if an inky spider had danced a jig. On the other there were ordinary words.

"What does it say?" Bill asked.

"Where is the bus, the train, the airport," Jenny read out. "Can I have a ticket, two tickets, three tickets – "

"Can't it make up its mind?" Bill asked, puzzled.

"It's trying to teach itself English," Jenny explained. "It's a phrase book for foreigners. It must be a tourist."

"From Mexico?" Bill asked.

"No," Jenny said. "I don't think so."

"Where, then?"

"Somewhere else. How should I know?"

"Ask it."

"Where do you come from?" Jenny asked the Thing very loudly.

"I do not remember," the Thing said. It put its hand on its head, and winced. "Hurt. Where is doctor, hospital, ambulance? Thank you, please."

It sat on the ground and covered its face with its hands. "Can you help me?" it sobbed.

They shook their heads and crept away, leaving the Thing alone in the woods, weeping.

Chapter 4

THEIR MOTHER WAS in the kitchen, making cakes to put in the freezer. Her face was pink, and she smelled of warm cherry pie and chocolate sponge and apple flan.

"Get that dog out of here!" she cried, as soon as she saw them.

"But, Mum, he was brave. He came back," Bill said. "There was this Thing in the woods. It was awful. It had

38

purple eyes and green hair and feet like a chicken."

"Did it, dear? That's nice," Mrs Clarke said vaguely. "Jenny, pass me that wire stand, there's a good girl."

"Mum, you're not listening," Bill complained.

"What, dear? Jenny, if you stuff yourself with sultanas, you won't have any room for your lunch – "

"Mum!"

"What is it, Bill?" she asked, but turned away to take a baking tray out of the oven.

"*Mum!*" Bill shouted. "Listen to me."

Mrs Clarke dropped the baking tray on the floor. A rock cake rolled over and came to rest at Fortissimo's feet. He ate it gratefully.

"Now look what you made me do,"

Mrs Clarke said. "Now he's spitting it out all over the floor. Filthy beast."

"It was too hot for him. I'll give him some water – "

"Not in here, you won't! Out! Go on, out, all three of you! You can take his bowl with you."

They went out into the garden.

Their father was sitting in the deckchair, reading his paper. The lawnmower was on the tufty grass beside him, like an unfulfilled promise.

"I was just going to start," he said, without looking round.

"It's only us," Jenny said. "Dad, we saw a funny Thing in the woods – "

"It was as tall as you," Bill cried. "Taller."

"And as thin as string."

"It had purple eyes and green hair – "

"And a green fur coat."

"Let me guess," their father said. "I know. It was that boy next door."

"Dad, it wasn't. It wasn't human – "

"That's him. Not human."

"Please don't try to be funny, Dad," Jenny said coldly. "It wasn't Tom Bryant. I don't know what it was. A

sort of foreigner. It couldn't speak
English properly."

"Oh, a tourist," their father said.
"Lot of them about."

"It wasn't an ordinary tourist,"
Jenny said slowly. "You should've seen
it. It didn't look like anything on
earth."

"Ah, it must've come from another planet then," their father said cheerfully. "Mars, that's it. It was a Martian." He winked at Jenny.

She did not smile. She wished Dad would be serious sometimes. She and Bill weren't babies any more. Or at least, *she* wasn't, she thought, looking

at her brother scornfully. His eyes were round and shining.

"A Martian," he repeated, and began chanting under his breath. "I've seen a Martian! I've seen a Martian!"

He was quite happy now he knew what the Thing was. He looked forward to telling his friends about it. They were meeting that afternoon in Johnny Connor's garden. Bill did not like Johnny Connor quite as much as he liked his other friends. In fact, he sometimes didn't like him one little bit. Sometimes Johnny Connor behaved more like an enemy than a friend.

I bet he's never seen a Martian, Bill thought. I should think he'd want to hear all about it. He won't tell me to shut up and stop being stupid now. They'll all want to hear about it.

He smiled. He saw himself in the

middle of an admiring circle of friends,
for once the most important person
there.

Chapter 5

IN JOHNNY CONNOR'S garden, the children gathered round Bill Clarke. They were not listening in wonder to his tale. They were laughing at him.

Johnny Connor didn't believe Bill had seen a Martian. He said there were no such things as Martians. There wasn't any life on Mars, he said, not so much as a mouse. Nor a beetle. Not even an ant.

"There's only red dust and rock and gas swirling about," he said. "The Americans, or the Russians or someone, sent a camera up on a shuttle

and it took photographs. There was
nothing there, see? It's a dead planet.
So you're a liar."

"I'm not! I did see a Martian! I
did!"

"Liar! Liar! Your pants are on fire!"
his friends chanted. "Your bottom is
burning, you'll have to jump higher!"

"I'm not a liar! It's true!" he
shouted, close to tears. "I did see one
and Jenny saw it too!"

But Jenny was not there to support him. She had gone out with her own friends. And nobody here would believe him.

"What did it look like?" one of them asked.

"It had purple eyes and green hair and feet like a chicken. *It did!*" he said, as everyone laughed.

"A chicken!" they cried, and began

running around, flapping their elbows up and down like wings, and clucking.

"Did it lay an egg?" a voice asked. It was Johnny's older sister, Ada. She was a tall, thin girl with a lemon-drop face. "A space egg. A speckled space egg especially for silly Billy's supper on Saturday. Bet you can't say that without spitting."

Bill did not answer. He kept his lips pressed tightly together so that he wouldn't cry.

"There *are* Martians," she whispered, coming close to him. Her breath smelled of vinegar. "They didn't tell people in case there was a panic, see? There are Martians and do you know what they do? They eat little boys. Fat little boys like you. They come in the night and gobble them up

out of their beds. And wipe their
greasy mouths on the sheets. That's
what Martians do."

"I don't believe you," Bill said.
"You're making it up."

"I'm not. It's true."

"You're a liar!" he shouted, and ran off.

He was very quiet when he got home. He didn't eat much of his supper. He refused to go to bed. He said he was never going to bed again.

"What's the matter, darling?" his mother asked.

"Nothing," he said, and began to cry.

"I expect it was that funny-looking Thing we saw in the woods," Jenny said. "The one you said was a Martian, Dad."

"Really, Joe, did you have to – " Mrs Clarke began, and Mr Clarke interrupted quickly. "It was only a joke. Bill didn't take me seriously. Did you, Bill?"

Bill sniffed, and didn't answer.

"A big boy like you doesn't believe

in space monsters," Mr Clarke went on hopefully.

"Ada Connor says there are space monsters and she's ten," Bill muttered.

"Ada Connor is a silly, spiteful girl," his mother said. "She was teasing you. She used to frighten her brother half out of his wits when he was small."

"Did she? How?" Bill asked, sounding wistful, as if he wished he could frighten Johnny Connor too.

"Don't worry, Bill," his father said. "I won't let anything hurt you. You'll be safe in bed, I'll see to that. If any

Martians come here, I'll chase them away with my new chopper."

"Promise?" Bill asked.

"I promise," Mr Clarke said. "And you know me. I always keep my promises."

Chapter 6

JENNY LAY IN her small room,
listening. It was windy outside. A twig
was tapping at the window.

Tap . . . tappit . . . tap-tap . . .

It's only a twig, she told herself, and
turned to face the wall.

"Eek, eek, eek."

Jenny sat up. She wasn't afraid. Dad
wouldn't let the Martian hurt her. She
got out of bed and crossed to the
window. She drew back the curtains.

The Thing was sitting in the apple
tree, looking in at her. Its face was
dripping with tears like a squeezed
lemon.

"Excuse me very much," it said.
"Where is café, snack bar,
restaurant?"

It was hungry. Its face was thin and
sad.

Jenny tried to think where it could
go. There was the King's Head Hotel,

but it was very posh. She didn't think they would let the Thing in, not without shoes. One look at those bird-like toes, and they might even send for the police.

There was the Chinese take-away in Archway Road –

"What do you like to eat?" she asked.

"Food," it said, and licked its lips with a long grey tongue.

"Have you any money?"

"Money?" it asked, puzzled. It began leafing through its book, muttering, "Money, money, money . . ."

"Oh, never mind," she said. "It's probably shut now. I'll see what I can get you. Can you eat bread and sardines and cold rice pudding?"

It looked doubtful.

"You can't afford to be choosy," she said crossly. "I'll do my best. Wait there."

She went out on to the landing and began creeping down the stairs. The sitting room door opened suddenly, and the sound of music billowed out. Fortissimo barked and she heard her father say, "All right, all right. Just a minute. Let me get my shoes on."

He was going to take Fortissimo out. Down to the pub probably. That meant he'd go out the back way, under the apple tree –

She fled silently back to her room and went over to the window.

"Go away! Quick! Go away!" she cried. "Dad's coming out with our dog. If he sees you, he'll chop you up!"

"Chop?" the Thing repeated. It looked down at its book and smiled. "Two lamb chops," it said hopefully, "with chips."

"No! Not that sort of chop. Go away. Shoo! Scram!" Jenny said, flapping her hands at it. "Or Dad will hurt you. *Hurt*, d'you understand? Hit. Wham. Bonk."

It disappeared from the window. She heard a thud and saw it galloping off across the lawn like an untidy broomstick. It clambered over the fence. Then it was gone.

Jenny waited. She saw her father and Fortissimo come out of the house. They walked under the apple tree. Fortissimo's nose quivered. He began sniffing and barking and pulling at his lead. He was trying to tell her father about the Thing, but her father wouldn't listen.

"Shut up, you silly dog," he said. "You'll wake the children."

Jenny watched them go out through the garden gate. Then she shut her window and fastened the catch. She drew her curtains tight, and went back to bed.

All night in her dreams she heard the Thing crying in the woods. "Eek, eek, eek."

Chapter 7

"WHY DON'T YOU take Fortissimo out now," their mother said next morning. "They said on the radio it's going to rain this afternoon."

Jenny and Bill put Fortissimo on his lead and went outside. It was very hot and clammy. They stood on the pavement and looked down towards the dark woods.

"The Thing was hungry," Jenny

said. "It came to my window last night. And cried."

"It's always crying." Bill sounded a little scornful. But then he frowned and asked anxiously, "Do you think it eats boys?"

"Of course not," Jenny said, laughing. "It eats food. It said it did."

"Tigers eat boys. And girls too," Bill added, for he hated being laughed at and didn't see why Jenny shouldn't worry too. "We're food for tigers."

"It's not a tiger, it's a Martian. Anyway, you haven't asked me what I've got in this bag." She was holding a brown paper bag in her hand, and she began swinging it backwards and forwards.

"What?"

"Bread and honey and chocolate

and a banana. Food for the Martian.
Much nicer than a tough little boy.
You're not frightened of going to the
woods, are you?"

"No," Bill said. "Not exactly."

He looked very small and pale.

"Oh, all right," Jenny said, smiling
at him. "Let's go to the park. We can
eat the food ourselves."

Fortissimo didn't want to go to the park. He wasn't allowed to chase the ducks there, or dig in the flower beds or join in the picnics on the lawns. Besides he was hot, and the shadowy woods looked cool and inviting. When Jenny tried to pull him towards the park, he sat down. He was a big dog. A heavy dog. Jenny pulled and Bill pushed. Fortissimo did not move.

"A battle," a voice said. "Ten pence on your dog to win."

They looked round. It was Johnny Connor and his thin, lemon-drop sister Ada.

"Poor doggie," Ada said, with false sympathy. "Aren't you going to take him walkies in the woods today? I wonder why not."

"They're afraid of that Martian

chicken," Johnny crowed, and began flapping his elbows up and down.

"They're only babies," Ada said, very tall and superior.

"I'm older than your brother," Jenny cried angrily.

"In years. Not in sense. We're not afraid to walk in the woods, are we, Johnny?"

"No," her brother replied. "And if we meet your Martian hen, we'll wring its neck and have it for dinner."

Laughing, they ran down the road and went into the dark wood.

"Dinner?" the Thing asked hopefully.

Bill and Jenny looked round. It was standing looking over the garden wall of the house opposite. "Which way to dinner, much please?" it said.

Its face, framed in roses, looked very thin and dim now. Its purple eyes had faded to a wishy-washy pink. Its hair was as lank as old grass. Its voice was faint and rasping, like a fingernail scratching paper.

"Here's some food for you," Jenny said, holding out the paper bag at arm's length. Fortissimo barked eagerly but she shushed him. "Not for you. For this – um – this gentleman. Or lady," she added uncertainly.

The Thing took the bag from her and opened it. It bent its face down and sniffed, its face wrinkling up like a concertina. Then it opened its mouth so wide that its other features were squeezed out of sight, pushed the paper bag inside and shut its mouth again with some difficulty. Its purple eyes bulged.

"It'll choke," Bill whispered.

The Martian swallowed, smiled at them and then belched, putting its hand politely in front of its mouth.

"Pardon rude noise," it said. "How much was dinner, price, bill?"

"Ten pence," Bill said quickly before Jenny, who was sometimes foolishly generous, could say it was a gift.

The Thing felt in its left pocket. It felt in its right pocket. Then it

unbuttoned its green fur coat and searched in some hidden pockets, wrapping its thin arms round its body and pushing its fingers into the lining of its coat. Then it began to cry. "Eek, eek, eek."

"Now you've upset it," Jenny whispered crossly. "Don't cry," she said kindly to the Martian. "It was a present. We don't want any money."

But the Martian began crying even louder, tears spurting from its eyes until the front of its fur coat was all wet and bedraggled, and the roses around it were freckled with tears.

"Eek, eek, eek, ah-oo-oo!" it howled.

And Fortissimo threw back his head in sympathy and joined in. "Oo-oo-oo!"

No sooner had the echoes died away
than someone screamed in the woods.
Loudly. Shrilly. Fortissimo barked.
The screams answered him, coming
nearer. The leaves shook.

Johnny and Ada Connor burst out of
the woods. Their faces were white,
their eyes staring and their mouths

gaping wide. They would have run straight past if Jenny hadn't grabbed hold of Ada's arm.

"What's the matter? What are you screaming for? The Martian isn't even in the woods. It's here."

Ada looked at her wildly, and then past her to where the Martian was standing, on the other side of the low garden wall, framed in roses.

"Oh no! Johnny, there's another monster! Look, another monster!"

She jerked her arm out of Jenny's hand and fled after her brother down the sunlit pavement.

"What is monster, can you tell please?" the Thing asked, blinking the tears from its eyes.

"Don't take any notice," Jenny said. "She's a nasty, rude girl."

"Monster is girl?"

"A monster is a great horrible thing," Bill explained. "Like this." He put his tongue out, rolled his eyes and wiggled his fingers in his ears.

Fortissimo was barking again. Staring at the woods, his brown eyes bulging. His tail wagged timidly and then stopped.

There was a crashing in the woods. A banging and snapping of twigs. Suddenly huge voices, loud as a brass band, rang out, calling "Toz! Toz! SKA WACK? TOZ!"

The Martian's purple eyes shone like ripe plums in the sunlight. Its smile was so wide that it nearly sliced off the top of its head.

"Mippa! Dappa!" it cried happily.

It took a step forwards, then it stopped and turned to Jenny.

"My name is Toz," it told her. It

put its little yellow book in her hands.
"For you. From Toz. Present, gift,
wrapping paper. Goodbye very much."

Jenny's hand was shaking so much
that she nearly dropped the book. For
the woods were moving, swaying,
coming towards them – four thin grey
tree trunks strode over the shadowed
ground like giant legs.

They were giant legs! Now they bent
in the middle, legs with huge knobbly
knees. There were green fur coats as
big as bushes, two large grey faces

descending through the leaves, smiling . . .

Toz ran into their arms.

They hugged him. They kissed his green head and his grey cheeks. One of them took out a large white handkerchief and wiped away his tears.

"Why, it's only a little Thing," Jenny whispered. "A child. A lost child."

Toz was walking off with the two large Martians or whatever they were. They were talking together in their strange speech. Then Toz said quite clearly, "Mippa, Dappa, I see monsters this day. One, two, three. Girl monster. Boy monster. Rude monster on four legs. I speak the English good, yes?"

Bill and Jenny watched the strange

family until they were out of sight. The woods were very quiet.

"He thought *we* were monsters," Bill said indignantly.

"He must've meant Johnny and Ada," Jenny assured him. "And poor old Fortissimo."

She looked at her present, turning the pages slowly. "We are friends, you are friends, they are friends," she read out.

Suddenly there was a bright green light. A whoosh. Something shot up into the air like a luminous melon. It grew smaller and smaller. Now it was the size of a pea. Now a seed. Now it was gone.

They stared up at the empty sky in silence.

"D'you think Johnny Connor saw that?" Bill asked at last.

"Dunno. Might've done."

"Anyway, he saw Toz, didn't he? He cried and ran away, didn't he? Johnny Connor's the baby, not me. Toz was my friend."

"Yes," Jenny said, still gazing up at the empty sky.

"You are lucky," Bill said wistfully. "He gave you his book. He must've liked you best."

Jenny looked at him and smiled. She was a generous girl.

"He meant it for both of us," she said.

RADIO RESCUE

John Escott

Mia is enjoying her holiday with her father by the seaside, away from her mother who is always criticizing her for not reading and writing well. But Mia's reading difficulties lead her into all sorts of trouble when she ignores the Danger sign.

MICHAEL AND THE JUMBLE-SALE CAT

Marjorie Newman

Michael lives in the children's home with his best friend Lee and his precious jumble-sale cat. One day Jenny, his social worker, asks if he'd like to live with a new family and Michael is thrown into confusion, but when the day arrives for him to leave the children's home he is both sad and glad. His new family turn out to be very special indeed!

DUMBELLINA

Brough Girling

What could be worse than the thought of moving house, changing school and leaving all your friends behind? When her Mum announces they are moving, Rebecca feels totally miserable – until she meets Dumbellina, the iron fairy.

HOT HENRIETTA AND NAILBITERS UNITED
Jules and Effin Older

Henrietta is a nailbiter. She eats nails for breakfast, she eats nails for lunch, she eats nails for supper. However hard she tries to stop, she just keeps on nibbling and to make things worse, her brother Hank teases her about her crazy ideas for a cure! Will Henrietta succeed in her attempt to have glamorous nails?

COMPUTER FOR CHARLIE
Joy Allen

In these two adventures, Charlie gets the blame when his Dad's computer program is erased and he nearly misses school summer camp! Luckily, the real culprit is found in time and Charlie gets to go – but will he be picked for the County Rovers Team? Find out in this very funny read.

JASON BROWN – FROG
Len Gurd

At first, Jason Brown is so surprised to be offered a wish that he can't think of anything to ask for. Then he remembers the misery of being afraid of water, and all he wants is to be able to swim – to swim as well as the frog who is granting him the wish. His wish comes true, but with startling results – webbed feet and green skin take a bit of getting used to . . .

THE RAILWAY CAT AND THE HORSE
Phyllis Arkle

Alfie and his friends are very curious to learn that a valuable horse is going to be delivered to their station. Could it be a racehorse, they wonder? They soon find out that it's no ordinary horse, but one that's going to need very special treatment.

THE HODGEHEG
Dick King-Smith

The story of Max, the hedgehog who becomes a hodgeheg, who becomes a hero. The hedgehog family of Number 5A are a happy bunch but they dream of reaching the Park across the road. Unfortunately, a very busy road lies between them and their goal and no one has found a way to cross it in safety. No one, that is, until the determined young Max decides to solve the problem once and for all . . .

STICK TO IT, CHARLIE
Joy Allen

In these two 'Charlie' adventures, Charlie meets a new friend and finds a new interest – playing the piano. The new friend proves his worth when Charlie and the gang find themselves in a tight spot. As for the piano – well, even football comes second place!